For
Mum, Dad
and
Lolly Dog.

First published in Great Britain in 2015 by Andersen Press Ltd.,
20 Vauxhall Bridge Road, London SW1V 2SA.
This paperback edition first published in 2016.
Copyright © Kim Geyer, 2015.
The rights of Kim Geyer to be identified as the author and illustrator
of this work have been asserted by her in accordance with the
Copyright, Designs and Patents Act, 1988.
Colour separated in Switzerland by Photolitho AG, Zurich.
Printed and bound in China.

1   3   5   7   9   10   8   6   4   2

British Library Cataloguing in Publication Data available. ISBN 978 1 78344 207 2

Go to Sleep, Monty!

KIM GEYER

ANDERSEN PRESS

Max loved his toy dog, Snuffly Poo.
They had been together since Max was a baby.

Now that Max was a big boy,
Mum and Dad said he could have a real puppy.
"But you'll have to look after him," they said.

Max went with his parents
to choose the puppy.

He loved Monty!

Monty was big, but he was still a baby. Max tried really hard to look after him, but it wasn't easy...

"Bad boy, Monty!" "Oh, no!"

That night, Max put Monty in his very own puppy bed, and covered him with his very own puppy blanket.

"Go to sleep, Monty," said Max.

But Monty did not sleep.
He whimpered and he wept.

"Now, now, don't be
afraid, Monty," said Max,
tucking him up tightly.
"Nighty, night."

But Monty did not sleep.
He scratched at the door and
he barked and he howled.

"Ok, Monty," said Max. "You can sleep in here just for tonight."

But Monty did not sleep. He jumped on Max's bed and he slobbered and he dribbled and he drooled.

Max sang him a song,
did a little dance
and made shadow
puppets on the wall.

But still Monty did not sleep.
He went into the kitchen.

uh oh!

He **howled** and he **hooted**, and he **yapped** and he **yelped**, and he **wailed** and he **whined**, and he **sniffled** and he **snuffled**, and he...

... **peed** on the **floor!**

Max loved Monty very much, but he wished,
just a little bit, that Monty would go to sleep.
There must be something that would help.
Suddenly Max had a **brilliant idea!**

"I'll lend you Snuffly Poo, Monty," said Max.
"He always helped me go to sleep when I was a baby."
But Monty had other ideas...

Max carried Monty's basket back into the living room, and Monty hid under his blanket.

uh oh!

Then Max felt sorry. He hadn't meant to shout at Monty.

But, he was very, **very** sleepy now.

He yawned and rubbed his tired eyes.

Max gave Monty a big cuddle and climbed

into the puppy bed to have a think,

just for a moment, just for a while, just until ...

Max was fast asleep. "Nighty, night," thought Monty.

Kim once had a dog called Lolly, who was just like Monty. When Lolly was a puppy she would not go to sleep either, until a little girl called Amy snuggled up with her in the puppy bed. There they both slept happily - for a few hours anyway!

Nighty, night.